Many Moons

JAMES THURBER

Many Moons

Illustrated by MARC SIMONT

A Harcourt Brace Contemporary Classic
Harcourt Brace & Company
San Diego   New York   London

First Harcourt Brace Paperback edition 1998

The Library of Congress has cataloged the hardcover edition as follows:
Thurber, James, 1894–1961.
Many moons/by James Thurber; illustrated by Marc Simont.
p. cm.
"Harcourt Brace Contemporary Classic."
Summary: Though many try, only the court jester is able to fulfill
Princess Lenore's wish for the moon.
ISBN 0-15-251872-X
ISBN 0-15-201895-6 pb
[1. Princesses—Fiction. 2. Moon—Fiction.] I. Simont, Marc, ill. II. Title.
PZ7.T422Man   1990
[E]—dc20   89-36465

F E D C B A

Printed in Singapore

The illustrations in this book were done in Winsor & Newton watercolors
on Arches paper.
The display and text type were set in Diotima by Harcourt Brace & Company
Photocomposition Center, San Diego, California.
Color separations by Bright Arts, Ltd., Hong Kong
Printed and bound by Tien Wah Press, Singapore
This book was printed on Arctic matte paper.
Production supervision by Stanley Redfern and Jane Van Gelder
Designed by Camilla Filancia

Introduction

As a woman who fancies herself to be one who lives actively in the present and who is open to change, I was startled by my difficulty in accepting HBJ's idea of "reinterpreting" *Many Moons.*

I spent my days, and some nights, struggling with "old" vs. "new," "tradition" vs. "change." After a few weeks of this "wiggle-waggle," as my Grandmother Thurber called bouts of indecision, I made a decision. I decided I was stuck and I turned to my children and grandchildren.

I should have consulted them in the first place. They are not so old and not yet so attached to things past as it turns out I am. They are wise. They all expressed their appreciation for the original version of *Many Moons* but the family consensus was that a new artist's point of view could be exciting.

When Marc Simont agreed to be the "reinterpreter," any anxiety I had left disappeared. Marc is family. He knows my father's works and has illustrated two of them. He knew my father personally. (Marc has drawn a dash of Thurber himself into one of the story's characters. I won't say which one, but I'll bet you can guess!) We are delighted to have Marc's illustrations. His paint jars are full of color and wit and, when it's needed, just the right amount of sweetness.

So, here's to change! I hope those of you who remember the old will cherish it as you join us in celebrating this beautiful new edition. For those of you who are new to *Many Moons,* welcome to a very special story.

— ROSEMARY THURBER

ONCE UPON A TIME, in a kingdom by the sea, there
lived a little Princess named Lenore. She was ten years old,
going on eleven. One day Lenore fell ill of a surfeit of
raspberry tarts and took to her bed.

The Royal Physician came to see her and took her
temperature and felt her pulse and made her stick out her
tongue. The Royal Physician was worried. He sent for the
King, Lenore's father, and the King came to see her.

"I will get you anything your heart desires," the King said.
"Is there anything your heart desires?"

"Yes," said the Princess. "I want the moon. If I can have the
moon, I will be well again."

Now the King had a great many wise men who always got
for him anything he wanted, so he told his daughter that
she could have the moon. Then he went to the throne room
and pulled a bell cord, three long pulls and a short pull, and
presently the Lord High Chamberlain came into the room.

The Lord High Chamberlain was a large, fat man who
wore thick glasses which made his eyes seem twice as big as
they really were. This made the Lord High Chamberlain
seem twice as wise as he really was.

"I want you to get the moon," said the King. "The Princess Lenore wants the moon. If she can have the moon, she will get well again."

"The moon?" exclaimed the Lord High Chamberlain, his eyes widening. This made him look four times as wise as he really was.

"Yes, the moon," said the King. "M-o-o-n, moon. Get it tonight, tomorrow at the latest."

The Lord High Chamberlain wiped his forehead with a handkerchief and then blew his nose loudly. "I have got a great many things for you in my time, your Majesty," he said. "It just happens that I have with me a list of the things I have got for you in my time." He pulled a long scroll of parchment out of his pocket.

"Let me see, now." He glanced at the list, frowning. "I have got ivory, apes, and peacocks, rubies, opals, and emeralds, black orchids, pink elephants, and blue poodles, gold bugs, scarabs, and flies in amber, hummingbirds' tongues, angels' feathers, and unicorns' horns, giants, midgets, and mermaids, frankincense, ambergris, and myrrh, troubadours, minstrels, and dancing women, a pound of butter, two dozen eggs, and a sack of sugar—sorry, my wife wrote that in there."

"I don't remember any blue poodles," said the King.

"It says blue poodles right here on the list, and they are checked off with a little check mark," said the Lord High Chamberlain. "So there must have been blue poodles. You just forget."

"Never mind the blue poodles," said the King. "What I want now is the moon."

"I have sent as far as Samarkand and Araby and Zanzibar to get things for you, your Majesty," said the Lord High Chamberlain. "But the moon is out of the question. It is 35,000 miles away and it is bigger than the room the Princess lies in. Furthermore, it is made of molten copper. I cannot get the moon for you. Blue poodles, yes; the moon, no."

The King flew into a rage and told the Lord High Chamberlain to leave the room and to send the Royal Wizard to the throne room.

The Royal Wizard was a little, thin man with a long face. He wore a high red peaked hat covered with silver stars, and a long blue robe covered with golden owls. His face grew very pale when the King told him that he wanted the moon for his little daughter, and that he expected the Royal Wizard to get it.

"I have worked a great deal of magic for you in my time, your Majesty," said the Royal Wizard. "As a matter of fact, I just happen to have in my pocket a list of the wizardries I have performed for you." He drew a paper from a deep pocket of his robe. "It begins: 'Dear Royal Wizard: I am returning herewith the so-called philosopher's stone which you claimed—' no, that isn't it." The Royal Wizard brought a long scroll of parchment from another pocket of his robe. "Here it is," he said. "Now, let's see. I have squeezed blood out of turnips for you, and turnips out of blood. I have produced rabbits out of silk hats, and silk hats out of rabbits. I have conjured up flowers, tambourines, and doves out of nowhere, and nowhere out of flowers, tambourines, and doves. I have brought you divining rods, magic wands, and crystal spheres in which to behold the future. I have compounded philters, unguents, and potions, to cure heartbreak, surfeit, and ringing in the ears. I have made you my own special mixture of wolfbane, nightshade, and eagles' tears, to ward off witches, demons, and things that go bump in the night. I have given you seven-league boots, the golden touch, and a cloak of invisibility—"

"It didn't work," said the King. "The cloak of invisibility didn't work."

"Yes, it did," said the Royal Wizard.

"No, it didn't," said the King. "I kept bumping into things, the same as ever."

"The cloak is supposed to make you invisible," said the Royal Wizard. "It is not supposed to keep you from bumping into things."

"All I know is, I kept bumping into things," said the King.

The Royal Wizard looked at his list again. "I got you," he said, "horns from Elfland, sand from the Sandman, and gold from the rainbow. Also a spool of thread, a paper of needles, and a lump of beeswax—sorry, those are things my wife wrote down for me to get her."

ouch!!

"What I want you to do now," said the King, "is to get me the moon. The Princess Lenore wants the moon, and when she gets it, she will be well again."

"Nobody can get the moon," said the Royal Wizard. "It is 150,000 miles away, and it is made of green cheese, and it is twice as big as this palace."

The King flew into another rage and sent the Royal Wizard back to his cave. Then he rang a gong and summoned the Royal Mathematician.

The Royal Mathematician was a bald-headed, nearsighted man, with a skullcap on his head and a pencil behind each ear. He wore a black suit with white numbers on it.

"I don't want to hear a long list of all the things you have figured out for me since 1907," the King said to him. "I want you to figure out right now how to get the moon for the Princess Lenore. When she gets the moon, she will be well again."

"I am glad you mentioned all the things I have figured out for you since 1907," said the Royal Mathematician. "It so happens that I have a list of them with me."

He pulled a long scroll of parchment out of a pocket and looked at it. "Now, let me see. I have figured out for you the distance between the horns of a dilemma, night and day, and A and Z. I have computed how far is Up, how long it takes to get to Away, and what becomes of Gone. I have discovered the length of the sea serpent, the price of the priceless, and the square of the hippopotamus. I know where you are when you are at Sixes and Sevens, how much Is you have to have to make an Are, and how many birds you can catch with the salt in the ocean—187,796,132, if it would interest you to know."

"There aren't that many birds," said the King.

"I didn't say there were," said the Royal Mathematician. "I said if there were."

"I don't want to hear about seven hundred million imaginary birds," said the King. "I want you to get the moon for the Princess Lenore."

"The moon is 300,000 miles away," said the Royal Mathematician. "It is round and flat like a coin, only it is made of asbestos, and it is half the size of this kingdom. Furthermore, it is pasted on the sky. Nobody can get the moon."

The King flew into still another rage and sent the Royal Mathematician away. Then he rang for the Court Jester.

The Jester came bounding into the throne room in his motley and his cap and bells, and sat at the foot of the throne.

"What can I do for you, your Majesty?" asked the Court Jester.

"Nobody can do anything for me," said the King
mournfully. "The Princess Lenore wants the moon, and she
cannot be well till she gets it, but nobody can get it for her.
Every time I ask anybody for the moon, it gets larger and
farther away. There is nothing you can do for me except
play on your lute. Something sad."

"How big do they say the moon is," asked the Court Jester, "and how far away?"

"The Lord High Chamberlain says it is 35,000 miles away, and bigger than the Princess Lenore's room," said the King. "The Royal Wizard says it is 150,000 miles away, and twice as big as this palace. The Royal Mathematician says it is 300,000 miles away, and half the size of this kingdom."

The Court Jester strummed on his lute for a little while. "They are all wise men," he said, "and so they must all be right. If they are all right, then the moon must be just as large and as far away as each person thinks it is. The thing to do is find out how big the Princess Lenore thinks it is, and how far away."

"I never thought of that," said the King.

"I will go and ask her, your Majesty," said the Court Jester. And he crept softly into the little girl's room.

The Princess Lenore was awake, and she was glad to see the Court Jester, but her face was very pale and her voice very weak.

"Have you brought the moon to me?" she asked.

"Not yet," said the Court Jester, "but I will get it for you right away. How big do you think it is?"

"It is just a little smaller than my thumbnail," she said, "for when I hold my thumbnail up at the moon, it just covers it."

"And how far away is it?" asked the Court Jester.

"It is not as high as the big tree outside my window," said the Princess, "for sometimes it gets caught in the top branches."

"It will be very easy to get the moon for you," said the
Court Jester. "I will climb the tree tonight when it gets caught
in the top branches and bring it to you."

Then he thought of something else. "What is the moon
made of, Princess?" he asked.

"Oh," she said, "it's made of gold, of course, silly."

The Court Jester left the Princess Lenore's room and went to see the Royal Goldsmith. He had the Royal Goldsmith make a tiny round golden moon just a little smaller than the thumbnail of the Princess Lenore. Then he had him string it on a golden chain so the Princess could wear it around her neck.

"What is this thing I have made?" asked the Royal Goldsmith when he had finished it.

"You have made the moon," said the Court Jester. "That is the moon."

"But the moon," said the Royal Goldsmith, "is 500,000 miles away and is made of bronze and is round like a marble."

"That's what you think," said the Court Jester as he went away with the moon.

The Court Jester took the moon to the Princess Lenore,
and she was overjoyed. The next day she was well again and
could get up and go out in the gardens to play.

But the King's worries were not yet over. He knew that the moon would shine in the sky again that night, and he did not want the Princess Lenore to see it. If she did, she would know that the moon she wore on a chain around her neck was not the real moon.

So the King sent for the Lord High Chamberlain and said, "We must keep the Princess Lenore from seeing the moon when it shines in the sky tonight. Think of something."

The Lord High Chamberlain tapped his forehead with his fingers thoughtfully and said, "I know just the thing. We can make some dark glasses for the Princess Lenore. We can make them so dark that she will not be able to see anything at all through them. Then she will not be able to see the moon when it shines in the sky."

This made the King very angry, and he shook his head from side to side. "If she wore dark glasses, she would bump into things," he said, "and then she would be ill again." So he sent the Lord High Chamberlain away and called the Royal Wizard.

"We must hide the moon," said the King, "so that the Princess Lenore will not see it when it shines in the sky tonight. How are we going to do that?"

The Royal Wizard stood on his hands
and then he stood on his head
and then he stood
on his feet again.

"I know what we can do," he said. "We can stretch some black velvet curtains on poles. The curtains will cover all the palace gardens like a circus tent, and the Princess Lenore will not be able to see through them, so she will not see the moon in the sky."

The King was so angry at this that he waved his arms around. "Black velvet curtains would keep out the air," he said. "The Princess Lenore would not be able to breathe, and she would be ill again." So he sent the Royal Wizard away and summoned the Royal Mathematician.

"We must do something," said the King, "so that the Princess Lenore will not see the moon when it shines in the sky tonight. If you know so much, figure out a way to do that."

The Royal Mathematician walked around in a circle, and then he walked around in a square, and then he stood still. "I have it!" he said.

"We can set off fireworks in the gardens every night. We will make a lot of silver fountains and golden cascades, and when they go off, they will fill the sky with so many sparks that it will be as light as day and the Princess Lenore will not be able to see the moon."

The King flew into such a rage that he began jumping up and down. "Fireworks would keep the Princess Lenore awake," he said. "She would not get any sleep at all and she would be ill again." So the King sent the Royal Mathematician away.

When he looked up again, it was dark outside and he saw
the bright rim of the moon just peeping over the horizon.
He jumped up in a great fright and rang for the Court Jester.
The Court Jester came bounding into the room and sat
down at the foot of the throne.

"What can I do for you, your Majesty?" he asked.

"Nobody can do anything for me," said the King mournfully.
"The moon is coming up again. It will shine into the Princess

Lenore's bedroom, and she will know it is still in the sky and that she does not wear it on a golden chain around her neck. Play me something on your lute, something very sad, for when the Princess sees the moon, she will be ill again."

The Court Jester strummed on his lute. "What do your wise men say?" he asked.

"They can think of no way to hide the moon that will not make the Princess Lenore ill," said the King.

The Court Jester played another song, very softly. "Your wise men know everything," he said, "and if they cannot hide the moon, then it cannot be hidden."

The King put his head in his hands again and sighed.

Suddenly he jumped up from his throne and pointed to the windows. "Look!" he cried. "The moon is already shining into the Princess Lenore's bedroom. Who can explain how the moon can be shining in the sky when it is hanging on a golden chain around her neck?"

The Court Jester stopped playing on his lute. "Who could explain how to get the moon when your wise men said it was too large and too far away? It was the Princess Lenore. Therefore the Princess Lenore is wiser than your wise men and knows more about the moon than they do. So I will ask *her.*" And before the King could stop him, the Court Jester slipped quietly out of the throne room and up the wide marble staircase to the Princess Lenore's bedroom.

The Princess was lying in bed, but she was wide awake and she was looking out the window at the moon shining in the sky. Shining in her hand was the moon the Court Jester had got for her. He looked very sad, and there seemed to be tears in his eyes.

"Tell me, Princess Lenore," he said mournfully, "how can the moon be shining in the sky when it is hanging on a golden chain around your neck?"

The Princess looked at him and laughed. "That is easy, silly," she said. "When I lose a tooth, a new one grows in its place, doesn't it?"

"Of course," said the Court Jester. "And when the unicorn loses his horn in the forest, a new one grows in the middle of his forehead."

"That is right," said the Princess. "And when the Royal Gardener cuts the flowers in the garden, other flowers come to take their place."

"I should have thought of that," said the Court Jester, "for it is the same way with the daylight."

"And it is the same way with the moon," said the Princess Lenore. "I guess it is the same way with everything." Her voice became very low and faded away, and the Court Jester saw that she was asleep. Gently he tucked the covers in around the sleeping Princess.

But before he left the room, he went over to the window
and winked at the moon, for it seemed to the Court Jester
that the moon had winked at him.